D1338620

C016659336

The Deal of a Lifetime

A few words before the rest of the words

This is a short story about what you would be prepared to sacrifice in order to save a life. If it was not only your future on the line, but also your past. Not only the places you are going, but the footprints you have left behind. If it was all of it, all of you, who would you give yourself up for?

I wrote this story late one night shortly before Christmas in 2016. My wife and children were sleeping a few arm lengths away. I was very tired; it had been a long and strange year, and I had been thinking a lot about the choices families make. Everyday, everywhere, we go down one road or another. We play around; we stay at home; we fall in love and fall asleep right next to each other. We discover we need someone to sweep us off our feet to realize what time really is.

So I tried to tell a story about that.

It was published in the local newspaper of my home-town, Helsingborg, in the southernmost part of Sweden. All the locations in the story are real – I went to school around the corner from the hospital, and the bar where the characters drink is owned and run by childhood friends of mine. I've got very drunk there on several occasions. If you're ever around Helsingborg, I highly recommend it.

I live six hundred kilometres further north now, in Stockholm, with my family. So, in retrospect, I think this story was not just about how I felt about love and death that night I was sitting on the floor next to the bed my wife and our kids were sleeping in, but also about my feelings for the place where I grew up. Maybe all people have that feeling deep down, that your home-town is something you can never really escape, but can never really go home to, either. Because it's not home anymore. We're not trying to make peace with it. Not with the streets and bricks of it. Just with the person we were back then. And maybe forgive ourselves for everything we thought we would become and didn't.

Maybe you will find this to be a strange story, I don't know. It's not very long, so at least it will be over quickly in that case. But I hope my younger self would have read it and found it to be . . . well . . . not horrible. I think he and I could have gone for a beer. Talked about choices. I would have shown him pictures of my family and he would have said, 'Alright. You did alright.'

Anyway, this is the story. Thank you for taking the time to read it.

With love,

Fredrik Backman

The Deal of a Lifetime

A novella

FREDRIK BACKMAN

Translated by Alice Menzies

MICHAEL JOSEPH
an imprint of
PENGUIN BOOKS

MICHAEL JOSEPH

UK | USA | Canada | Ireland | Australia
India | New Zealand | South Africa

Michael Joseph is part of the Penguin Random House group of companies
whose addresses can be found at global.penguinrandomhouse.com

Published by arrangement with the Salomonsson Agency
First published in Sweden by Helsingborgs Dagblad 2016
Published in the United States by Atria Books 2017
Published in Great Britain by Michael Joseph 2018
001

Printed in China by C&C offset Printing Co., Ltd.

A CIP catalogue record for this book is available from the British Library

ISBN: 978–0–241–35951–8

www.greenpenguin.co.uk

MIX
Paper from
responsible sources
FSC® C018179

Penguin Random House is committed to a
sustainable future for our business, our readers
and our planet. This book is made from Forest
Stewardship Council® certified paper.

Hi. It's your dad. You'll be waking up soon, it's Christmas Eve morning in Helsingborg, and I've killed a person. That's not how fairy tales usually begin, I know. But I took a life. Does it make a difference if you know whose it was?

Maybe not. Most of us so desperately want to believe that every heart which stops beating is missed equally. If we're asked, 'Are all lives worth the same?' the majority of us will reply with a resounding 'Yes!' But only until someone points to a person we love and asks: 'What about that life?'

Does it make a difference if I killed a good person? A loved person? A valuable life?

If it was a child?

She was five. I met her a week ago. There was a small red chair in the hospital TV room, it was hers. It wasn't red when she arrived, but she could see that it wanted to be. It took twenty-two boxes of crayons but that didn't matter, she could afford it, everyone here gave her crayons all the time. As though she could draw away her illness, colour away the needles and the drugs. She knew that wasn't possible, of course, she was a smart kid, but she pretended for their sakes. So she spent her days drawing on paper, because it made all the adults happy. And at night, she coloured in the chair. Because it really wanted to be red.

She had a soft toy, a rabbit. She called it 'Babbit.' When she first learned to speak, the adults thought she was calling it 'Babbit' because she couldn't say 'Rabbit.' But she called it Babbit because Babbit was its name. That shouldn't be so hard to understand, really, even for an adult. Babbit got scared sometimes, and then it got to sit on the red chair. It might not be clinically proven that sitting on a red chair makes you less scared, but Babbit didn't know that.

The girl sat on the floor next to Babbit, patting its paw and telling it stories. One night, I was hidden around a corner in the corridor and I heard her say: 'I'm going to die soon, Babbit. Everyone dies, it's just that most people will die in maybe a hundred thousand years but I might die already tomorrow.' She added, in a whisper: 'I hope it's not tomorrow.'

Then she suddenly looked up in fear, glanced around as though she had heard footsteps in the corridor. She quickly grabbed Babbit and whispered good night to the red chair. 'It's her! She's coming!' the girl hissed, running towards her room, hiding herself under the covers next to her mother.

I ran too. I've been running all my life. Because every night, a woman in a thick, grey, knitted jumper walks the hospital's corridors. She carries a folder. She has all our names written inside.

t's Christmas Eve, and by the time you wake up the snow will probably have melted. Snow never lasts very long in Helsingborg. It's the only place I know where the wind comes at an angle from below, like it's frisking you. Where the umbrellas protect you better if you hold them upside down. I was born here but I've never got used to it; Helsingborg and I will never find peace. Maybe everyone feels that way about their hometown: the place we're from never apologizes, never admits that it was wrong about us. It just sits there, at the end of the motorway, whispering: 'You might be all rich and powerful now. And maybe you do come home with expensive watches and fancy clothes. But you can't fool me, because I know who you really are. You're just a scared little boy.'

I met death by the side of my wrecked car last

night, after the accident. My blood was everywhere. The woman in the grey jumper was standing next to me with a disapproving look on her face and she said: 'You shouldn't be here.' I was so scared of her, because I'm a winner, a survivor. And all survivors are scared of death. That's why we're still here. My face was cut to shreds, my shoulder out of joint, and I was trapped inside 1.5 million kronors' worth of steel and technology.

When I saw the woman, I shouted, 'Take someone else! I can give you someone else to kill!'

But she just leaned forward, looked disappointed, and said: 'It doesn't work like that. I don't make the decisions. I just look after the logistics and the transportation.'

'For who? For God or the Devil, or . . . someone else?' I sobbed.

She sighed. 'I stay out of the politics. I just do my job. Now give me my folder.'

It wasn't the car crash that brought me to the hospital, I was there long before that. Cancer. I'd met the girl for the first time six days earlier, when I was smoking on the fire escape so the nurses wouldn't see me. They went on and on about smoking, as though it would have time to kill me.

The door to the corridor was ajar, and I could hear the girl talking to her mother in the TV room. They played the same game every night; when the hospital was so quiet that you could hear the snowflakes bouncing against the windows like good-night kisses, the mother whispered to the girl: 'What are you going to be when you grow up?'

The girl knew the game was for her mother's sake, but she pretended it was for hers. She laughed as she said, 'doctor' and 'engineeeer,' plus her perennial favorite: 'space hunter.'

Once the mother fell asleep in an armchair, the girl stayed where she was, colouring in the chair which wanted to be red and talking to Babbit whose name was that. 'Is it cold on death?' she asked Babbit. But Babbit didn't know. So the girl packed thick gloves in her backpack, just to be on the safe side.

She spotted me through the glass. She wasn't scared, I remember being furious at her parents for that. What kind of adult doesn't raise their kid to be terrified of a strange, forty-five-year-old, chain-smoking bloke who's staring at her from a fire escape? But this girl wasn't scared. She waved. I waved back. She grabbed Babbit's paw, came over to the door and spoke through the crack.

'Do you have cancer too?'

'Yes,' I replied. Because that was the truth.

'Are you famous? You're in a picture in Mummy's newspaper.'

'Yes,' I replied. Because that was also the truth. The papers wrote about my money, no one knew I was ill yet, but I'm the kind of person whose diagnosis will make the news. I'm not an ordinary person, everyone will hear about it when I die. When five-year-old girls die, no one writes about that, there aren't any memorials in the evening papers, their feet are still too small, they haven't had time to make anyone care about their footsteps yet. But people care about me because of what I'll leave behind, what I've built and achieved, businesses and properties and assets. Money isn't money to me, not like it is to you. I save and calculate and don't worry about it. It's nothing but points for me, just a measure of my success.

'It's not the same cancer you have,' I said to the girl. Because that was my only consolation in the diagnosis. That the doctor had apologetically explained: 'You have a very, very unusual type of cancer.'

I don't even get cancer like you people.

The girl blinked firmly and asked: 'Is it cold on death?'

'I don't know,' I said.

I should have said something else. Something bigger. But I'm not that man. So I just dropped my cigarette and mumbled: 'You should stop drawing on the furniture.'

I know what you're thinking: what a bastard I am. And you're right. But the vast majority of successful people don't become bastards, we were bastards long before. That's why we've been successful.

'You're allowed to draw on the furniture when you have cancer,' the girl suddenly exclaimed with a shrug. 'No one says anything.'

I don't know what it was about that, but I started to laugh. When had I last done that? She laughed too. Then she and Babbit ran off to their room.

t's so easy to kill someone, all a person like me needs is a car and a few seconds. Because people like you trust me, you drive thousands of kilos of metal at hundreds of kilometres an hour, hurtling through the darkness with the people you love most sleeping in the backseat, and when someone like me approaches from the opposite direction, you trust that I don't have bad brakes. That I'm not looking for my phone between the seats, not driving too fast, not drifting between lanes because I'm blinking the tears from my eyes. That I'm not sitting on the slip road to the 111 with my headlights out, just waiting for a lorry. You trust me. That I'm not drunk. That I'm not going to kill you.

The woman with the grey sweater pulled me out of the wreckage this morning. She wiped my blood from her folder.

'Kill someone . . . else,' I begged.

She took a resigned breath through her nose.

'It doesn't work like that. I don't have that kind of influence. I can't just swap a death for a death. I have to swap a life for a life.'

'Do it, then!' I screamed.

The woman shook her head sadly, reached out and pulled a cigarette from my breast pocket. It was bent, but not broken. She smoked it in two long drags.

'I've actually given up,' she said defensively.

I lay bleeding on the ground and pointed to the folder.

'Is my name in there?'

'Everyone's is.'

'What do you mean, *a life for a life*?'

She groaned.

'You really are an idiot. You always have been.'

At one point in time, you were mine. My son.

The girl at the hospital reminded me of you. Something happened when you were born. You cried so loudly, and it was the first time it had happened to me: the first time I'd felt pain for someone else. I couldn't stay with someone who had that kind of power over me.

Every parent will take five minutes in the car outside the house from time to time, just sitting there. Just breathing and gathering the strength to head back inside to all of their responsibilities. The suffocating expectation of being good, coping. Every parent will take ten seconds in the stairwell occasionally, key in hand, not putting it in the lock. I was honest, I only waited a moment before I ran. I spent your entire childhood travelling. You were the girl's age when you asked what I did. I told you I made money. You said everyone did that. I said, 'No, the majority of people just survive, they think their things have a value but nothing does. Things only have a price, based on expectation, and I do business with that. The only thing of value on Earth is time. One second will always be a second, there's no negotiating with that.'

You despise me now, because I've devoted all my seconds to my work. But I have, at least, devoted them to something. What have your friends' parents devoted their lives to? Barbecues and rounds of golf? Charter holidays and TV shows? What will they leave behind?

You hate me now, but you were once mine. You once sat on my lap and were terrified of the starry sky. Someone had told you that the stars aren't really above us but below, and that the earth spun so quickly that if you were small and light you could easily fall off, straight into all that darkness. The porch door was open, your mother was listening to Leonard Cohen, so I told you that we actually lived deep in a cozy grotto and that the sky was like a stone covering the opening. 'Then what are the stars?' you asked, and I told you they were cracks, through which the light could trickle in. Then I said that your eyes were the same thing, to me. Tiny, tiny cracks, through which the light could trickle out. You laughed so loudly then. Have you ever laughed like that since? I laughed too. I, who had wanted to live a life high above everyone else, ended up with a son who would rather live deep beneath the surface.

In the living room, your mother turned up the volume and danced, laughing, on the other side of the window. You crawled higher in my lap. We were a family then, albeit fleetingly. I belonged to you both, for a moment or two.

I know you wished you had an ordinary father. One who didn't travel, wasn't famous, one who would have been happy with just two eyes on him: yours. You never wanted to say your surname and hear, 'Sorry, but is your dad . . . ?' But I was too important for that. I didn't take

you to school, didn't hold your hand, didn't help you blow out your birthday candles, I never fell asleep in your bed, halfway through our fourth bedtime story, with your cheek on my collarbone. But you'll have everything that everyone else longs for: Wealth. Freedom. I abandoned you, but at least I abandoned you at the top of the hierarchy of needs.

But you don't care about that, do you? You're your mother's son. She was smarter than me, I never quite forgave her for that. She also felt more than me, that was her weakness, and it meant I could hurt her with words. You might not remember when she left me, you were still so small, but the truth is that I didn't even notice. I came home after a trip and it took me two days to realize that neither of you were there.

Several years later, when you were eleven or twelve, the two of you had a huge argument about something and you took a bus to my house in the middle of the night and said you wanted to live with me. I said no. You were completely beside yourself, sobbing and crying on the rug in my hallway, screaming that it wasn't fair.

I looked you in the eye and said: 'Life isn't fair.'

You bit your lip. Lowered your eyes and replied: 'Lucky for you.'

You might have stopped being mine that day, I don't know. Maybe that's when I lost you. If that's the case, I was wrong. If that's the case, life is fair.

Four nights ago, the girl knocked on the window again.

'Do you want to play?' she asked.

'What?' I said.

'I'm bored. Do you want to play?'

I told her she should go to bed. Because I'm the person you think I am, the kind of person who says no when a dying five-year-old wants to play. She and Babbit went off towards her room, but the girl turned around and looked at me and asked: 'Are you brave too?'

'What?'

'Everyone always says I'm so brave.'

Her eyelids fluttered. So I replied honestly: 'Don't be brave. If you're scared, be scared. All survivors are.'

'Are you? Of the woman with the folder?'

I took a calm drag on my cigarette, nodded slowly.

'Me too,' said the girl.

She and Babbit walked towards her room. I don't know what happened then. Maybe I cracked, making all the light spill out. Or in. I'm not evil, even I understand that cancer should have an age limit. So I opened my mouth and said: 'Not tonight. I'll stay here and keep watch, so she doesn't come tonight.'

The girl smiled then.

The next morning, I was sitting awake on the floor in the corridor. I heard the girl and her mother playing a new game. The mother asked, 'Who do you want to invite to your next birthday party?' even though there wouldn't be a next one. And the girl played along, reeled off the names of everyone she loved. It's a long list when you're five. That morning, I was on it.

'm an egotist, you learnt that early on. Your mother once screamed that I'm the kind of person who doesn't have any equals, I only have people above me that I want something from and people beneath me who I trample on. She was right, so I kept going until there was no one left above me.

But just how big is my egotism? You know that I can buy and sell everything, but would I clamber over dead bodies? Would I kill someone?

I had a brother. I've never told you that. He was dead when we were born. Maybe there was only room for one of us on this earth, and I wanted it more. I clambered over my brother in the womb. I was a winner, even then.

The woman with the folder was there, at the hospital. I've seen the pictures. Sometimes, when my mother drank alone at night, she fell asleep too drunk to remember to hide them. The woman was everywhere in those photos, an out of focus figure outside windows, a blur in the corridors. In one from the day before our birth, she was standing in the queue behind my parents at a petrol station. Mum was heavily pregnant. Dad was laughing in that picture. I never saw him do that. Throughout my life, he only ever smiled.

When I was five, I saw the woman with the folder by some train tracks. I was about to cross when she leapt forward from the other side and shouted something. I stopped dead, astonished. The train appeared a second later, thundering by so close that I fell over. By the time it had passed, she was gone.

When I was fifteen, my best friend and I were playing on the rocks by the sea in Kullaberg and halfway up we passed a woman in a grey sweater. 'Be careful, these rocks are treacherous when it rains,' she mumbled. I didn't recognize her until she was already gone.

It started raining half an hour later, and my best friend fell headlong. The rain was still falling during his funeral, as though it never planned to stop. I saw the woman as I was leaving the church, she was standing beneath an umbrella in the square, but the rain was still flecking her cheeks, the way it only does in Helsingborg.

When my dad got sick, I saw her outside his room in the care home, on his last night. I came out of the toilet, she didn't notice me. She was wearing the same grey sweater, writing something in her folder with a black pencil. Then she went into his room and never came out again. Dad was dead the next morning.

When my mum got sick, I was working abroad. We spoke on the phone, she was so weak when she whispered: 'The doctor says everything looks normal.' So that I wouldn't worry about her dying a dramatic death. My parents always wanted everything to be like normal. Ever since my brother died, they just wanted to be like everyone else. Maybe that's why I became exceptional, out of sheer obstinacy. Mum passed away during the night, I hired an appraiser to go through her flat and her possessions; he sent me photos. In one of them, from the bedroom, there was a black pencil on the floor. By the time I got home, it was gone. Mum's slippers were in the hallway, and there were small clumps of grey wool on their soles.

failed with you. Fathers are meant to teach their sons about life, but you were a disappointment.

You called me on my birthday last autumn, I was forty-five. You had just turned twenty. You told me that you'd got a job in the old Tivoli building. The city had moved the entire building right across the square to make room for new private flats. You said the word 'private' with such disgust, because we're so different. You see history, I see development, you see nostalgia, I see weakness. I could have given you a job, could have given you hundreds of jobs, but you wanted to be a bartender at Vinylbaren, in a building that had been ready to fall down even when it was a steamboat station four generations earlier. I bluntly asked you whether you were happy. Because I am who I am. And you replied: 'It's good enough,

Dad. Good enough.' Because you knew I hated that phrase. You were always someone who could be happy. You don't know how much of a blessing that is.

Maybe it was your mother who forced you to call; I think she suspected I was sick, but you invited me down to the bar. You said they served *smørrebrød* in the café; you remembered that I always used to eat it when you and I took the ferry to Denmark at Christmas when you were small. Your mother had nagged me to do something special with you, at least once a year, I think you know that. But I couldn't sit still and talk, I needed to be on the way somewhere, and you got travel sick in the car. So we liked the ferry, both of us, me the way there and you the way back. I loved leaving everything behind, but you loved standing out on deck and watching Helsingborg appear on the horizon. The way home, the silhouette of something you recognized. You loved it.

I sat in my car in Hamntorget last autumn, saw you

through the window of the bar. You were making cock-tails and making people laugh. I didn't go in, I was afraid I would end up telling you that I had cancer. I wouldn't have been able to deal with your compassion. And I was drunk, of course, so I remembered the steps outside the house where you and your mother lived, and all the times you had sat there waiting for me when I didn't turn up like I'd promised. All the occasions I'd wasted your time. I remembered the ferries at Christmas, always early in the morning so that we would get home in time for me to spend the rest of the day drinking. Our last trip was when you were fourteen, I taught you to play poker in a basement bar in Helsingør, showed you how to identify the losers at a table: weak men with strong schnapps. I taught you to capitalize on those who couldn't understand the game. You won six hundred kronor. I wanted to keep playing, but you gave me a pleading look and said, 'Six hundred's good enough, Dad.'

You stopped at a jewellery shop on the way back to the ferry and bought some earrings with the money. It took me a whole year to realize that they weren't for some girl you were trying to charm. They were for your mother.

You never played poker again.

I failed with you. I tried to make you tough. You ended up kind.

Late last night, at the hospital, the woman with the folder came walking down the corridor. She stopped when she saw me. I didn't run. I remembered all the times I had seen her before. When she took my brother away. When she took my best friend. When she took my parents. I wasn't going to be scared anymore, I'd keep that power at least, down to the last moment.

'I know who you are,' I said, without a single tremor in my voice. 'You're death.'

The woman frowned and looked deeply, deeply offended. 'I'm not death,' she muttered. 'I'm *not* my job.'

That knocked the air out of me. I'll admit it. It's not what you expect to hear at a moment like that.

The woman's eyebrows lowered as she repeated: 'I'm not death. I just do the picking up and dropping off.'

'I – ' I began, but she interrupted me.

'You're so self-obsessed that you think I've been chasing you all your life. But I've been looking out for you. Of all the idiots I could have picked as my favorite . . .' She massaged her temples.

'Fa . . . favorite?' I stuttered.

She reached out and touched my shoulder. Her fingers were cold, they moved down towards my breast pocket and took a cigarette. She lit it, clutched her folder tight. Maybe it was just the smoke, but a lonely tear ran down her cheek as she whispered: 'It's against the rules for us to have favorites. It makes us dangerous, if we do. But sometimes . . . sometimes we have bad days at work too. You screamed so loudly when I came to get your brother, and I turned around and happened to look you in the eye. We're not meant to do that.'

My voice broke when I asked: 'Did you know . . . everything I've become, everything I've achieved . . . did you know? Was that why you took my brother instead of me?' She shook her head. 'It doesn't work like that. We don't know the future, we just do our job. But I made a mistake with you. I looked you in the eye and it . . . hurt. We're not meant to hurt.'

'Did I kill my brother?' I sniffed.

'No,' she said.

I sobbed despairingly. 'Then why did you take him? Why do you take everyone I love?'

She gently placed her hand in my hair. Whispered: 'It's not down to us who goes and who stays. That's why it's against the rules for us to hurt.'

When the doctor gave me the diagnosis, I didn't have an awakening, I just did my accounts. Everything I'd built, the footprints I've left behind. Weak people always look at people like me and say, 'He's rich, but is he *happy*?' As though that was a relevant measure of anything. Happiness is for children and animals, it doesn't have any biological function. Happy people don't create anything, their world is one without art and music and skyscrapers, without discoveries and innovations. All leaders, all of your heroes, they've been obsessed. Happy people don't get obsessed, they don't devote their lives to curing illnesses or making planes take off. The happy leave nothing behind. They live for the sake of living, they're only on earth as consumers. Not me.

But something happened. I walked along the beach

out by Råå, the morning after the diagnosis, and I saw two dogs running into the sea, playing in the waves. And I wondered: Have you ever been like that, as happy as they are? Could you be that happy? Would it be worth it?

The woman lifted her hand from my hair. She seemed almost ashamed.

'We're not meant to feel things. But I'm not . . . just my job. I have . . . interests too. I knit.'

She gestured to her grey sweater. I tried to nod appreciatively, because it felt like she expected it. She nodded back with smoke in her eyes. I took the deepest breath of my life.

'I know you're here to collect me now. And I'm ready to die,' I managed. As though it were a prayer. And then she said the one thing I feared even more: 'I'm not here for you. Not yet. You'll find out tomorrow that you're healthy. You'll live for a long while yet, you'll have time to achieve whatever you want.'

I trembled. Hugged myself like a child and sobbed. 'Then what are you doing here?'

'My job.'

She patted me gently on the cheek. Then she walked off down the corridor, stopped outside a door and opened her folder. Slowly pulled out a black pencil and crossed out a name. Then she opened the door to the girl's room.

The day before yesterday, I heard the girl and her mother arguing. The girl wanted to make a milk-carton dinosaur, but there wasn't time. The girl got angry, the mother cried. The girl stopped then, the corners of her mouth jumping over the despair leaving her eyes as though it was a skipping rope, and she held her mother's hand and said: 'Okay, then. But what about a game?'

They had one where they pretended to talk on the phone. The mother said she had been taken captive by pirates, that she was on her way to their secret island to help the pirates build a flying pirate ship, and in exchange they would sail her home again. The girl laughed and forced her mother to promise that they would build a milk-carton dinosaur *then*! After that, the girl explained that she was on a space ship with 'alianies.' 'Aliens,' her mother corrected her. 'Alianies,' the girl corrected. 'They've got mysterious machines with huge buttons and they stick wires into my arms and they have masks over their faces and uniforms that rustle and you can only see their heads. And they whisper, 'There there, there there, there there,' and then they count down from ten. And when they get to one you go to sleep. Even though you try not to!'

The girl fell silent, because the mother was crying then, even though it was just a game. So the girl whispered: 'The alianies will save me, Mummy. They're the best.'

The mother tried not to kiss her a million times. The nurses came and lifted the girl onto the rolling bed to take her to the operating theater. They passed mysterious machines with huge buttons. The girl had wires stuck to her arms and the alianies wore uniforms which rustled and masks over their faces and when they leaned over the edge of the bed all she could see was their heads. They whispered, 'There there, there there, there there,' and then counted down from ten. And when they got to one, the girl fell asleep. Even though she tried not to.

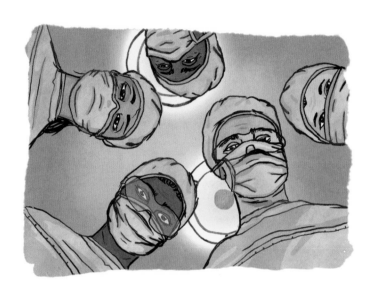

t's bloody awful to admit to yourself that you're not the kind of person you've always thought you were. All you normal people would have tried to save the child if you could, wouldn't you? Of course you would. So when the woman with the grey sweater opened the door to the girl's room, part of me cracked, because it turns out that I'm more normal than I thought. I shoved the woman, grabbed the folder, and then I ran. As though I were one of you.

My car was parked outside the hospital; the brake lights never came on. The wheels grappled for something to cling onto in the snow. I drove down Bergaliden towards town, and then took Strandvägen north, towards the sea. The most beautiful stretch in the world. I thundered between the trees by Sofiero Castle, towards the terraced houses in Laröd, and didn't slow down before I reached the 111. There, on the slip road to the bigger road, I stopped and turned off the headlights. As the lorry approached, I drove straight out. I don't remember the crash, just the pain in my ears and the light which washed over me as the steel crumpled like foil. And the blood, everywhere.

The woman dragged both me and the folder out of the wreck. When I shouted, 'I can give you some-one else to kill!' she realized that I meant myself. But it made no difference. She couldn't take a death for a death. Only a life for a life.

I lay there on the ground with all of Helsingborg's winds beneath my clothes, and she patiently explained: 'It's not enough for you to die. To make room for the girl's entire life, another life has to cease to exist. I have to delete its contents. So if you give your life, it'll disap-pear. You won't die, you'll never have existed. No one will remember you. You were never here.'

A life for a life. That's what it means.

That was why she brought me to you. She had to show me what I was giving up.

An hour ago, we were standing in Hamntorget watching you clean the bar through the window. 'You never get your child's attention back,' your mother once said. 'The time when they don't just listen to you to be nice, that time passes, it's the first thing to go.'

The woman stood beside me and pointed at you. 'If you give your life for the girl at the hospital, you'll never have been his.'

I blinked, out of step.

'If I die . . .'

'You won't die,' she corrected me. 'You'll be erased.'

'But . . . if I don't . . . If I've never . . .'

She wearily shook her head at my lack of understanding. 'Your son will still exist, but he'll have a different father. Everything you'll leave behind will still exist, but it'll have been built by someone else. Your footprints will vanish, you'll never have existed. You humans always think you're ready to give your lives, but only until you understand what that really involves. You're obsessed with your legacy, aren't you? You can't bear to die and be forgotten.'

I didn't answer for quite some time. I thought about whether you would have done it, given your life for someone else. You probably would. Because you're your mother's son, and she's already given a life. The one she could have lived if she hadn't lived for you and for me.

I turned to the woman. 'I've sat here watching him every evening since I got sick.'

She nodded. 'I know.'

I knew that she knew. I'd understood that much by now. 'Every night, I wondered whether it was possible to change a person.'

'What did you conclude?'

'That we are who we are.'

She started walking straight towards you then. I panicked. 'Where are you going?' I shouted.

'I need to be sure that you're sure,' she replied, crossing the car park and knocking on the door of Vinylbaren.

I ran after her and hissed: 'Can he see us?'

I don't know what I was expecting. The woman turned to me, mockingly raised one eyebrow and replied: 'I'm not a bloody ghost. Of course he can see us!'

When you opened the door, she muttered, 'I need a beer,' without paying any attention as you patiently – like your mother would have done – tried to explain that unfortunately the bar was closed. Then you saw me. I think both of our worlds probably came to a standstill right then.

You didn't say anything about my ripped suit, or the blood on my face, you'd seen me in a worse state before. The woman in the grey sweater ate smørrebrød and drank three beers in a row, but I asked for a coffee. I saw how happy that made you. We said very little, because there was too much I wanted to say. That's always when we fall silent. You wiped the bar and sorted the glasses, and I thought about the love in your hands. You've always touched the things you like as though they had a pulse. You cared about that bar, adored this town. The people and the buildings and the night as it approached over the Sound. Even the wind and the useless football team. This has always been your town in a way it never was for me; you never tried to find a life, you were in the right place from the start.

I told the woman in the grey sweater what you had told me: that they had moved the entire Tivoli building right across the square. That's what fathers do, they sit in front of their sons and tell their son's stories to a third person rather than letting them speak for themselves. The woman looked at me for intervals which were far too short between blinks.

'You don't care?' I asked.

'I really, really, really don't,' she replied.

And you laughed then. Loudly. It made me sing inside.

I asked questions, you answered. You told me that you had designed everything in the bar with respect for the building's history. It showed. I should have told you that. Not for your sake, because you won't remember any of this, but for mine. I should have told you I was proud.

You cleared everything away and I followed you, awkwardly, clutching my coffee cup. You turned around to take it, and our hands briefly overlapped. I felt your heart beat, right in the ends of your fingertips.

You glanced at the woman in the bar, she was reading the cocktail menu and had paused on one containing 'gin, lime, pastis, and triple sec.' Its name was *Corpse Reviver No. 3*. She laughed at that, and then you laughed too, though you found it funny for completely different reasons.

'I'm glad you've met someone who's . . . you know . . . your own age,' you said quietly to me.

I didn't know what to reply. So I didn't.

You smiled and kissed me on the cheek. 'Merry Christmas, Dad.'

My heart fell to the floor and you walked through the door into the kitchen. I couldn't bring myself to let you come back. A second is always a second; that's the one definitive value we have on earth. Everyone is always negotiating, all of the time. You're doing the deal of your life, every day. This was mine.

The woman drank the last of her beer. Picked up the folder from the bar. We went to the outdoor seating area; there's fierce competition for the most beautiful view in Helsingborg, but that particular place is so calm and confident. It doesn't need to show off, it knows its own beauty. The waves rolling in, the ferries anchored in the harbor, Denmark waiting on the other side of the water.

'How does this work?' I asked.

'We jump inwards,' the woman replied.

'Does it hurt?' I asked.

She nodded sadly.

'I'm scared,' I admitted, but she shook her head.

'You're not scared. You're just grieving. No one tells you humans that your sorrow feels like fear.'

'What are we grieving?'

'Time.'

I nodded towards the windows in the bar and whispered: 'Will he remember anything?'

She shook her head. 'Sometimes, for a second, he might feel like there's something missing. But . . . then . . .' She clicked her fingers.

'And the girl?'

'She'll live her life.'

'Will you keep watch over them?'

The woman nodded slowly. 'I've never liked the rules anyway.'

I buttoned my jacket. The wind was blowing at an angle from below. 'Is it cold . . . where we're going?' I asked.

But the woman didn't reply. She just handed me a pair of knitted gloves. They were grey, but there was a single thin red thread hanging from one of them. She pulled a small pair of scissors from one of her pockets and carefully cut it away. Then she held my hands as we jumped inwards. You'll never read this. You've never sat waiting on the steps outside your mother's house. I've never wasted your time.

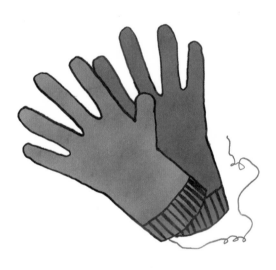

And as we jumped inwards, the woman with the folder and I, I saw Helsingborg as you've always seen it, for the briefest of moments. Like the silhouette of something you recognize. A home. It was our town then, finally, yours and mine.

And that was good enough.

You'll wake up soon. It's Christmas Eve morning. And I loved you.